WHISPERS OF THE MYSTICAL ISLES

G.E DWYNNIGAN

ISBN: 978-1-4467-7531-8

Dedication

To Our Dearest Lauren,

This book, "Whispers of the Mystical Isles," is a testament to the brilliance and magic that resides within you. From the very beginning, you've shown us that you are more than just a rocket scientist or a rock star—you are a force of nature, embracing both the light and dark with grace.

Dad, and the authors Your Mum & Friend E who are 'G.E DWYNNIGAN' have all played a part in crafting this tale, but it is your spirit and unique journey that have breathed life into its pages. Your fascination with crystals has inspired the Crystal Heist Rockstar in you—a harmony of power and wonder that knows no bounds.

Like a canvas adorned with many colours, you paint your world with vibrancy and curiosity. As you embark on your own path of independence, remember that you are a kaleidoscope of dreams, capable of creating beauty and magic wherever you go.

With this dedication, we honnor the spark that sets you apart—a beacon of uniqueness that ignites the hearts of those who know you. May "Whispers of the Mystical Isles" be a reminder of the boundless possibilities that lie before you.

Believe in yourself, embrace your journey, and let your soul dance with the mystical whispers of the Isles.

With all our love and admiration,
Dad, Mum & Family Friend E
xxx

Chapters

Poetic Whispers Of The Mystic Isles

In dreams' embrace, mysteries unfold,
Where magic and wonder, stories are told.
Follow Lauren's path, self-discovery's flight,
A symphony of dreams, woven in night.

With girlish charm and rock star's fire,
She dances 'twixt shadows, light's desire.
Crystals' secrets and beings of lore,
Within her soul's depths, magic does soar.

Past's echoes and futures unknown,
Guide her journey, courage is sown.
Resilience blooms, empowerment's grace,
Friendship's bond woven in time's embrace.

Protecting Isles mystical, she'll stand,
Whispers through ages, tales of the land.
Listen to your soul's symphony's song,
Unveil your uniqueness, rise, belong.

Infinite horizons, life's tapestry unfurls,
"Whispers of the Mystical Isles," dreams swirl.
Inspired and uplifted, enchanted heart's call,
Magical expedition, enchantment for all.

Step into the symphony, dreams anew,
Let the magic surround, and your spirit imbue.

The Leading Role - Lauren

Lauren is a remarkable young woman on a journey of self-discovery and empowerment. Raised in a loving Welsh and Irish family by her caring mum Gillian and her dad Nick, she exudes a unique blend of girlish charm and rock star individuality. With a heart that embraces both light and darkness, Lauren's multifaceted personality is a kaleidoscope of dreams and aspirations.

A lover of all things magical, Lauren's fascination with crystals and mythical creatures drives her to uncover the hidden secrets of the mystical Isles. As she prepares for a month of independence while her parents embark on their own adventure, Lauren's life takes a transformative turn. In her quest for identity, she finds strength in her grandparents' guidance—Nanny Susan and Grampy Charles—and the unwavering support and love from Gillian and Nick.

Throughout her odyssey, Lauren learns to embrace her dual nature, breaking free from societal norms to embrace her true self. As she bonds with mystical beings and harnesses the power of crystals, Lauren becomes a beacon of inspiration for those around her. Her friendships with both mortal and mystical allies strengthen, forming a powerful network of support on her journey.

As she delves deeper into the mysteries of the mystical Isles, Lauren discovers an ancient prophecy that hints at her unique destiny. Guided by whispers from ages past and present, she gains wisdom and insight that shapes her path and empowers her to face the malevolent forces threatening the mystical Isles.

Lauren's journey culminates in a symphony of self-discovery, where she harmonizes her various aspects into a powerful force of unity and acceptance. Through courage, resilience, and the belief in her own potential, Lauren proves that embracing her true self, with the love and encouragement of G and N, is the key to fulfilling her destiny and protecting the mystical Isles from darkness.

With a spirit that dances between the pink hues of girlish dreams and the dark depths of her rock star soul, Lauren's story resonates as a tale of empowerment, inspiration, and the magic that lies within us all.

A Journey Through the Mystical Isles

In the enchanting world of "Whispers of the Mystical Isles," embark on a mesmerizing tale that weaves magic, mystery, and self-discovery into a tapestry of wonder.

Meet Lauren, a spirited young woman with a heart that dances between the pink hues of girlish dreams and the deep shadows of her rock star soul. Raised in the embrace of her Welsh and Irish heritage, Lauren's journey of self-discovery takes flight as she prepares for a momentous month of independence while her parents, Nick, and Gill, set out on an adventure of their own.

As Lauren explores the realms of her dreams, she stumbles upon an extraordinary revelation—a secret society of enchanting beings, guardians of the mystical Isles that bridge the worlds of light and darkness. Guided by her fascination with all things magical, Lauren uncovers an ancient prophecy that hints at her unique destiny.

In her quest to embrace her true self, Lauren delves into the secrets of her ancestry and the power of crystals—an enigmatic force that resonates with her soul. Guided by the whispers of the mystical Isles, she learns to harness her latent abilities and forges a bond with creatures beyond imagination.

Yet, darkness lurks in the shadows, threatening the delicate balance of the mystical Isles. As Lauren grapples with her dual nature and the choices that shape her path, she finds solace in the wisdom of her grandparents, Nanny Susan and Grampy Charles, who have always supported her through thick and thin.

With her loyal companions, both mortal and mystical, by her side, Lauren embarks on a perilous adventure to protect the mystical Isles from an ancient and malevolent force. As she uncovers the truth of her lineage and the significance of her dual heritage, she finds the strength to confront her fears and embrace her destiny.

"Whispers of the Mystical Isles" is a spellbinding tale that weaves a tapestry of self-discovery, friendship, and courage. Join Lauren as she navigates the realms of magic and the depths of her own soul, uncovering the magic that lies within us all.

A Glimpse Into - Whispers Of The Mystical Isles

Dive into a symphony of dreams, where magic and wonder intertwine in the most unexpected ways. Follow Lauren, a spirited young woman on a journey of self-discovery, as she embarks on an odyssey that will not only resonate with her but also captivate the hearts of all who dare to follow her path.

In "Whispers of the Mystical Isles," Lauren's story is a celebration of the beauty of self-discovery and the power of embracing one's uniqueness. She is a kaleidoscope of dreams, a fusion of girlish charm and rock star soul, who dances between the light and dark with grace. As she delves into the secrets of crystals and mythical beings, she unveils the magic that lies within her very soul.

This enchanting tale weaves together the ancient echoes of the past and the promises of the future, guiding Lauren on a symphonic journey of courage, resilience, and empowerment. It is a narrative that paints a vivid tapestry of unity, acceptance, and the profound bond of friendship.

In Chapter 1, "The Call of Destiny," Lauren discovers an ancient prophecy that hints at her unique destiny and stumbles upon a secret society of enchanting beings who guard the mystical Isles.

Chapter 2, "Embracing the Shadows," sees Lauren exploring her dual nature, embracing both her girlish dreams and her rock star soul. She bonds with mystical creatures and harnesses the power of crystals.

Throughout Chapter 3, "The Rock Star Vampire," Lauren faces challenges that test her resolve, but her resilience shines through. She learns to balance light and shadow within herself and discovers the beauty in her unique identity.

As the journey unfolds in Chapter 4, "The Enchanted Crystal Cave," Lauren faces challenges that test her resolve, but her resilience shines through. She learns to balance light and shadow within herself and discovers the beauty in her unique identity.

In Chapter 5, "The Enigmatic Prophecy," the ancient prophecy reveals more secrets about Lauren's destiny, drawing her deeper into the mystical Isles' mysteries. Her bond with her companions strengthens, and they face obstacles together.

Chapter 6, "Tales of Past and Present," takes Lauren on a captivating exploration of the mystical Isles' past, connecting her to the rich history of her ancestors. Her understanding of her heritage grows, empowering her to face the challenges ahead.

In Chapter 7, "Whispers Across the Ages," Lauren's connection to the mystical Isles grows stronger, allowing her to communicate with beings from the past and present. Through these whispers, she gains wisdom and insight, guiding her towards her ultimate purpose.

The story approaches climax in Chapter 8, "The Symphony of Self," where Lauren discovers the true power within her—her ability to harmonize the diverse aspects of her identity into a symphony of self. With newfound courage, she faces the malevolent force threatening the mystical Isles.

In the final chapter, Chapter 9, " The Magical Odyssey" Lauren's journey comes full circle as she embraces her uniqueness and celebrates the magic that resides within her. This aspirational and thought-provoking ending reminds us of all to dare to dream and embrace the infinite possibilities that life offers.

Step into the symphony, and let your dreams awaken.

1

The Call Of Destiny

On a serene summer morning, the sun painted the sky with hues of orange and pink as gentle waves caressed the shores of Barry Island. Lauren stood at the water's edge, her heart aflutter with excitement and a tinge of nervousness. Today was a momentous day—one that marked the beginning of an extraordinary journey.

As the daughter of Gillian and Nick, Lauren was about to face a new chapter in her life—one that would challenge her, inspire her, and shape her into the woman she was destined to become. Her parents, Gillian, and Nick, were set to embark on a month-long adventure across the continents, exploring the vast wonders of Australia, New Zealand, and Indonesia. While they were away, Lauren would remain in Barry Island, her childhood home, for a month of independence.

The prospect of being on her own for an extended period both thrilled and intimidated Lauren. Though she had always been a spirited and independent soul, the idea of her parents being a world away filled her heart with a mixture of emotions. She knew this was an opportunity to spread her wings and discover the depths of her strength.

Lauren's journey of independence had already been set in motion. In the days leading up to her parents' departure, she had busied herself with preparations, both physical and emotional. Her room, typically adorned with a mixture of girly pink decorations and Gothic touches, reflected her multifaceted personality.

She sat on the edge of her bed, surrounded by shelves of crystals and trinkets collected from her many travels. Among her treasures were smooth pebbles and delicate seashells, souvenirs from far-off lands and cherished memories. Lauren's love for collecting transcended the material—it was a way for her to hold on to the moments that had shaped her journey thus far.

In the days leading up to the departure, Lauren reconnected with old friends and spent cherished moments with her family. She sought the company of her cousin Josh, whom she had always shared a special bond with, and her auntie Dawn, who had been a source of guidance and wisdom throughout her life.

One evening, as the sun dipped below the horizon, Lauren sat with her grandmother, Nanny Susan, reminiscing about the adventures they had shared over the years. Nanny Susan's gentle smile warmed Lauren's heart as she offered words of encouragement and reassurance.

"My dear Lauren, you have a heart of gold," Nanny Susan said, her eyes sparkling with love. "You have always had a way of connecting with others, especially with animals. Remember, your ability to understand and care for them is a rare gift."

Lauren nodded, her mind drifting to her days spent horse riding in the lush fields surrounding Barry Island. She had always felt an inexplicable bond with the magnificent creatures, and they responded to her with an uncanny understanding.

"Nanny, I sometimes wonder if my love for the supernatural and the macabre makes me strange," Lauren confessed, her fingers tracing the intricate patterns of a crystal pendant."

Nanny Susan chuckled softly, placing a comforting hand on Lauren's shoulder. "My dear, uniqueness is what makes you truly extraordinary. Embrace all aspects of yourself—the light and the shadows. It is this duality that makes you who you are."

As the days passed, Lauren felt a newfound sense of confidence within herself. She began to see her quirks and interests not as flaws, but as the facets of a beautiful gem—a gem that was uniquely her own.

The day of her parents' departure finally arrived, and as Lauren stood on the familiar shores of Barry Island, she felt a swell of emotions. Gillian and Nick embraced her tightly, promising to keep in touch throughout their travels.

"Lauren, you are capable of anything you set your mind to," Gillian said, her eyes filled with pride. "Remember, you have a whole network of support around you. If you ever need help or simply want to talk, we're just a call away."

Nick added with a smile, "You've always been our rock star, and now it's time for you to shine even brighter."

Lauren grinned, feeling a mix of excitement and trepidation. She watched as her parents' car disappeared into the distance, knowing that this was a journey that would change her in ways she couldn't yet comprehend.

As the sun dipped below the horizon, casting a golden glow over the island, Lauren felt a sense of peace wash over her. She knew that the days ahead would be filled with new experiences, challenges, and moments of self-discovery. With her parents' words echoing in her heart, she took a deep breath, ready to embrace the adventure that awaited her.

Lauren's journey to independence on Barry Island was a transformative experience that allowed her to discover her strength and independence in ways she never thought possible. Through the course of her month-long adventure, Lauren was able to reconnect with old friends, spend cherished moments with her family, and discover her love for the natural world. Her love for collecting had transcended the material and was a way for her to hold onto the moments that had shaped her journey thus far. With newfound confidence, Lauren saw her quirks and interests not as flaws but as the facets of a beautiful gem that was uniquely her own.

During her month of independence, Lauren spent her days hiking through the nearby woods, swimming in the ocean, and indulging in her love of literature. She also befriended locals, learned to cook new dishes, and discovered hidden gems throughout the island. Each moment was a step towards her self-discovery, and she relished in the sense of independence that came with it.

As she stood once again on the shores of Barry Island, Lauren felt a sense of accomplishment wash over her. She knew that the journey had been a transformative one, and that she had discovered her strength and independence in ways she never thought possible. As she looked out over the vast expanse of the ocean, Lauren felt a sense of clarity wash over her. She knew that the journey of self-discovery was ongoing—that there would always be new adventures to embark on and new horizons to explore. But with each step, she felt empowered, knowing that she could overcome any obstacle that came her way.

As Lauren stood on the shores of Barry Island, she felt a newfound sense of clarity and purpose. Her month-long adventure had been transformative, and she had discovered a newfound love for the natural world. Her time spent hiking through the nearby woods and swimming in the ocean had connected her with the environment in a way she had never experienced before.

But it wasn't just the beauty of nature that had captured Lauren's heart. She had also befriended locals who had welcomed her into their community with open arms. They had taught her to cook new dishes, introduced her to their favourite spots on the island, and shared stories of their own journeys of self-discovery.

Through these interactions, Lauren had come to realize that independence was not just about being alone—it was about building connections with others and discovering the world around her. Her time on Barry Island had given her a newfound appreciation for the beauty of life and the importance of relationships.

As she looked out at the vast expanse of the ocean, Lauren felt a sense of peace wash over her. She knew that her journey of self-discovery was far from over, but she was excited to see where it would take her next.

With newfound confidence and a heart full of love

Lauren took a deep breath and stepped forward into the next chapter of her extraordinary journey.

The moon rose high in the night sky, casting a silvery haze over the world. Shadows danced and whispered secrets, beckoning our hero deeper into the mystical realm. In the darkness, they discovered a hidden society of beings who lived in harmony with the shadows, harnessing their power for good. With each step, our hero embraced the unknown, their path illuminated by the enigmatic glow of destiny.

2

Embracing The Shadows

In the days that followed her parents' departure, Lauren felt a newfound sense of independence settling within her. The house seemed quieter, and yet, there was a serenity in the solitude that she had never experienced before. As the sun dipped below the horizon each evening, she found herself drawn to the attic—the secret sanctuary where she could explore her interests freely.

The attic was a treasure trove of forgotten relics and mementos, a time capsule of her childhood adventures. Among the dusty boxes, Lauren discovered an old diary she had started years ago—a testament to her fascination with the supernatural and the macabre. As she flipped through its pages, she couldn't help but smile at her younger self's vivid imagination.

With the diary in hand, Lauren sat cross-legged on the floor, a flickering candle casting dancing shadow around her. She began to write once again, pouring her thoughts and dreams onto the pages. She wrote of vampires, witches, and the mystical creatures that lived in the shadows of her mind.

The attic became her sanctuary—a place where she could be her true self without any judgments or expectations. She surrounded herself with crystals of various shapes and colours, feeling their energies infusing her soul with strength and clarity. Among them was a magnificent amethyst, her favourite crystal—one that resonated with her inner peace and spiritual growth.

Her crystal collection grew, each one carefully chosen based on its unique properties and healing qualities. She spent hours researching their meanings, learning about their abilities to soothe anxiety, enhance intuition, and balance energy. The crystals became her trusted companions, and she carried them with her wherever she went, feeling their comforting presence.

As days turned into weeks, Lauren ventured out into the world with newfound confidence. She reconnected with old friends, meeting up with Abby, Mariella, and her beloved cousins, Josh, Riley, and Ellie. Together, they strolled along the sandy shores of Barry Island, sharing laughter and memories of their youth.

One sunny afternoon, Lauren and her friends decided to explore the dense woods on the outskirts of the island. They hiked along narrow trails, the dense foliage creating an enchanting labyrinth. As they approached a clearing, they stumbled upon an ancient stone circle—a place shrouded in legends and mystery.

Lauren's heart skipped a beat as she gazed at the weathered stones. Something about the circle stirred a sense of familiarity within her. With her crystal pendant resting against her chest, she stepped inside the circle, feeling an electric surge of energy course through her veins.

As she closed her eyes, she imagined herself as a powerful witch—a keeper of ancient knowledge and arcane secrets. Her imagination took flight, and she could almost sense the presence of otherworldly beings surrounding her.

In that moment, Lauren understood that her fascination with the supernatural was more than mere curiosity—it was an intrinsic part of her being. She was not bound by the conventional norms of the world; rather, she was a conduit for the mystical and magical.

Her friends watched in awe as she embraced the circle, her aura radiating with an otherworldly glow. For a fleeting moment, Lauren felt a connection to the very fabric of the universe—an ancient force that transcended time and space.

As they left the stone circle, Lauren felt an overwhelming sense of empowerment. She knew that her interests and passions, which had once made her feel like an outsider, were her strengths—the very essence of her soul. She no longer sought validation from others because she had found her inner compass—a guiding light that led her toward her true path.

In the quiet of the evening, Lauren sat on the edge of the cliff overlooking the ocean, her feet dangling above the crashing waves below. The moon hung low in the sky, its silvery glow casting an ethereal spell over the world.

As she held her crystal pendant in her hand, she whispered to the night, "I am not afraid of my darkness. I embrace it, for it is a part of me, just as the light is. I am a rock star vampire, a witch with supernatural powers. And I am whole."

In that moment, the universe seemed to respond with a gentle embrace, as if acknowledging her truth. The stars twinkled in approval, and the wind carried her words to the farthest corners of the world.

With every passing day, Lauren's confidence grew. She no longer felt the need to conform to societal expectations or to fit into predefined boxes. Instead, she revelled in her uniqueness, knowing that her rock star vampire spirit and her connection to the supernatural were gifts that set her apart.

As the month of independence continued, Lauren's journey took her beyond the familiar boundaries of Barry Island. She ventured to the cliffs of Dover with Jake and his family, exploring new horizons, and discovering the joy of sharing experiences with loved ones.

Her time in Dover was filled with laughter, adventure, and moments of quiet introspection. The coastal landscapes seemed to mirror the depths of her soul, a perfect reflection of both the light and the shadows within her.

Together with Jake, Lauren explored the vibrant streets of Dover, their hands intertwined like a promise of shared adventures. They visited charming cafes and strolled along the chalk cliffs, the endless expanse of the sea stretching out before them.

In the evenings, they sat on the cliffs, watching the sun dip below the horizon, its fiery hues painting the sky with shades of gold and crimson. As darkness embraced the world, they revelled in the beauty of the night, gazing at the stars that seemed to dance just for them.

Throughout their journey, Lauren's fascination with crystals continued to deepen. She shared her knowledge with Jake, who listened with rapt attention as she explained the unique properties of each crystal she carried. Together, they discovered the magic in the smallest of things—the beauty in a moment shared, the wonder of nature's mysteries, and the strength in embracing their true selves.

As the month of independence ended, Lauren returned to Barry Island with a heart full of gratitude and a spirit ablaze with newfound wisdom. Her experiences had taught her that life was a journey of self-discovery—one that required embracing both her light and her darkness.

As she stood once again on the shores of Barry Island, she felt a sense of completeness. The month of independence had been a transformative odyssey—one that had shaped her into a woman who could navigate life's mysteries with grace and courage.

Lauren's parents returned from their travels, their eyes shining with pride as they embraced their daughter. They could see the metamorphosis that had taken place within her—the way she carried herself with confidence and a sense of purpose.

"You've grown into an incredible young woman," Gill said, her voice tinged with emotion.

Nick added with a smile,

"You're a rock star in every sense of the word."

Lauren beamed with pride, knowing that her journey of self-discovery was just the beginning. The magic of her rock star vampire spirit and her connection to the supernatural would guide her toward a future filled with endless possibilities.

Amidst the pulsating lights and thunderous applause of a crowded concert hall, our hero stumbled upon a charismatic figure. The enigmatic rock star possessed an otherworldly charm that drew people in like moths to a flame.

But behind the glamour and fame lay a secret – the rock star was a vampire, cursed to wander the earth seeking redemption. Intrigued by this duality, our hero embarked on a journey that would test their beliefs and challenge their understanding of good and evil.

3

The Rock Star Vampire

As the days turned into weeks, the magic of Lauren's journey continued to weave its spell. She returned to her daily routines, but something within her had shifted. The attic had become her haven—a place where she could escape the world and delve deeper into the mysteries that intrigued her.

In the silence of the attic, Lauren would lose herself in her diary, scribbling tales of rock star vampires, witches with mystical powers, and ancient prophecies. Her imagination took flight, and she felt as though she were living in a world of her own creation—a world where anything was possible.

Among the crystals that adorned the attic, one held a special place in Lauren's heart—the amethyst that she wore as a pendant. It seemed to emanate a soothing energy, guiding her on her quest for self-discovery. With its presence, she felt a deep sense of peace and assurance, as if the crystal itself was a guardian of her soul.

One evening, while gazing at the stars from her attic window, an idea struck her—a masquerade ball. It would be a celebration of uniqueness, a gathering of souls who embraced their quirks and embraced the extraordinary within themselves. She knew that such an event would be a way to bring together people who felt like outsiders, creating a haven where they could truly be themselves.

Enthralled by the idea, Lauren reached out to her friends and family, inviting them to the masquerade ball. She encouraged them to express their true selves through their costumes, to let their imaginations run wild, and to embrace the rock star vampires, witches, and supernatural beings they had always secretly admired.

The night of the masquerade ball arrived, and the air was charged with excitement and anticipation. Lauren stood at the entrance, dressed in a flowing black gown adorned with silver accents—a reflection of her rock star vampire alter ego. Her crystal pendant, the amethyst that had become a part of her identity, hung elegantly around her neck.

One by one, her friends and family arrived, their costumes a testament to their uniqueness. Abby had embraced her love for the mystical with a celestial-themed outfit, and Mariella donned a regal gown fit for a queen. Josh, Riley, and Ellie appeared as mischievous forest spirits, their faces adorned with intricate masks.

As the night unfolded, the masquerade ball became a spectacle of wonder and delight. The guests revelled in the freedom to express themselves fully—to embrace their dualities and their passions without fear of judgment.

With each passing hour, Lauren felt an overwhelming sense of gratitude. The masquerade ball had become a celebration of authenticity, a tribute to the power of embracing one's uniqueness. It was a night she would cherish forever—a night that reaffirmed her belief in the magic of self-discovery.

As the days turned into months, Lauren's journey of independence led her to explore new horizons. She immersed herself in her passion for arts and crafts, channelling her creativity into intricate creations that reflected her soul's desires.

One afternoon, she sat in her room, surrounded by an array of art supplies. Her fingers danced across the canvas, bringing to life a vibrant painting of a rock star vampire—a reflection of her inner spirit. The colours seemed to flow effortlessly from her brush, each stroke a manifestation of her thoughts and dreams.

As the painting neared completion, she added a final touch—a shimmering amethyst, embedded within the heart of the rock star vampire. It was a symbol of the power that resided within her—a reminder that she was a force to be reckoned with, a force that could conquer any challenge that came her way.

Her artistic journey also took her to the world of photography. Armed with her trusty camera, she captured the essence of her surroundings—the sunsets over Barry Island, the moonlit nights of Dover, and the breathtaking landscapes of Epsom. Through her lens, she found beauty in the ordinary, turning everyday moments into works of art.

Among her photography subjects were the horses she had once ridden with such grace. Although she no longer participated in horse shows, her bond with the magnificent creatures remained intact. They seemed to recognize the transformation within her, responding to her gentle demeanour with unwavering trust and affection.

Amid her exploration, Lauren also discovered the joys of cooking. She delved into the world of culinary delights, experimenting with recipes that combined her love for the macabre with her appreciation for the whimsical. Among her creations were cupcakes adorned with eerie designs and cookies shaped like mystical creatures.

As the seasons changed and the days grew shorter, Lauren found solace in the quietude of cemeteries—the serene resting places of the departed. She would visit these sacred grounds, wandering among the tombstones and paying her respects to those who had come before her.

Among the tombstones, she found inspiration for her art, capturing the beauty of decay and the cycle of life and death. In these moments of reflection, she felt a deep connection to the universe—a sense that life was both fleeting and eternal, a tapestry of souls woven together in a cosmic dance.

One evening, as Lauren strolled through a cemetery, she noticed a group of young children playing in the distance. Their laughter echoed through the air, juxtaposed against the sombre surroundings. Curiosity got the better of her, and she approached the children.

"Hello, little ones," she greeted them with a warm smile. "What brings you to this peaceful place?"

The children looked at her with wide eyes, their faces painted with awe. One of them, a little girl with golden curls, stepped forward.

"We're playing make-believe," the girl said, her voice tinged with excitement. "We're pretending to be witches and wizards!"

Lauren's heart swelled with delight. She joined the children in their imaginative game, casting spells and brewing imaginary potions. As the sun set, she bid the children farewell, feeling a profound sense of joy.

In that moment, Lauren understood that the world was a playground of possibilities—a canvas on which each soul could paint their unique story. She realized that she had a gift—the ability to inspire others to embrace their true selves, just as she had done throughout her journey of self-discovery.

As the days turned into years, Lauren's reputation as the rock star vampire with a heart of gold spread throughout Barry Island and beyond. Her photography and artwork garnered recognition, earning her a loyal following of admirers who resonated with her authenticity and her celebration of uniqueness.

She continued to host masquerade balls—events that became a symbol of unity and empowerment for those who attended. The masquerade balls were no longer just about Lauren's journey; they were a testament to the power of community—the strength that came from supporting one another in the pursuit of self-discovery.

With each passing day, Lauren's connection to the supernatural grew stronger. She delved deeper into the world of crystals, using their energies to heal and empower those around her. She became a mentor to young souls who felt lost, guiding them on their own journeys of self-discovery.

In her heart, Lauren knew that her journey of independence was not just a one-time event—it was a lifelong quest. She continued to explore new horizons, to embrace her ever-evolving self, and to celebrate the magic that resided within her.

And so, the tale of Lauren, the rock star vampire, continued—a symphony of

---

self-discovery, a celebration of uniqueness, and a testament to the power of embracing one's true self.

Amidst the pulsating lights and thunderous applause of a crowded concert hall, our hero stumbled upon a charismatic figure. The enigmatic rock star possessed an otherworldly charm that drew people in like moths to a flame. But behind the glamour and fame lay a secret – the rock star was a vampire, cursed to wander the earth seeking redemption.

Intrigued by this duality, our hero embarked on a journey that would test their beliefs and challenge their understanding of good and evil.

4

The Enchanted Crystal Cave

The days rolled on, and the enchanting aura of the masquerade ball still lingered in the hearts of those who had attended. In the aftermath of the event, Lauren received letters and messages from people across Barry Island and beyond, expressing their gratitude for the magical night that had ignited a spark of self-discovery within them.

Among the heartfelt messages was one from a mysterious sender—a person who simply signed their letter as "The Seeker." The letter spoke of a hidden realm, a place of wonder and mystique, where crystals held ancient secrets and magical energies. The Seeker invited Lauren to embark on a journey—an odyssey to the fabled "Enchanted Crystal Cave."

Intrigued and guided by her intuition, Lauren accepted the invitation. She sensed that this journey held the promise of unlocking even deeper mysteries within herself, and she longed to explore the possibilities that lay ahead.

As the day of departure approached, Lauren packed her bags with essentials—her art supplies, her camera, and, of course, her cherished crystals. Her parents, Gill, and Nick were both thrilled and concerned about her upcoming adventure.

"You must be careful, my love," Gill said, hugging her daughter tightly. "We may not fully understand what awaits you, but we trust that you'll follow your heart."

Nick nodded in agreement, adding, "You've grown into an extraordinary woman, and we know you have the strength to face whatever comes your way."

With her parents' blessings, Lauren set off on her journey, guided by the cryptic directions left by The Seeker. The path was shrouded in mystery, and as she walked deeper into the wilderness, she felt an otherworldly energy enveloping her. It was as if the universe itself was leading her to the hidden realm.

After days of traversing dense forests and crossing streams, Lauren finally arrived at the entrance to the Enchanted Crystal Cave. The cave's entrance glistened with crystals of various hues, as if welcoming her with open arms. She stepped inside, her heart pounding with anticipation.

The air within the cave was alive with energy—an ethereal glow that illuminated the walls adorned with crystals of every shape and size. The crystals sparkled like stars, casting a mesmerizing dance of light and shadows on the cave floor.

In the heart of the cave stood The Seeker—a figure cloaked in a flowing robe; their face obscured by a hood. The Seeker extended a hand, and Lauren felt an immediate connection—a recognition that they were kindred spirits on a shared quest of self-discovery.

"Welcome, dear Lauren," The Seeker said, their voice carrying a soothing resonance. "You have journeyed far to reach this sacred place—the domain of the crystals. Here, the secrets of the universe are whispered, and the depths of your soul are laid bare."

With a sense of reverence, Lauren approached The Seeker, feeling an ancient wisdom emanating from their presence. The Seeker motioned toward a pool of shimmering water, where crystals floated like blooming flowers.

"The crystals in this pool are attuned to your energy," The Seeker explained. "They will guide you through the reflections of your past, the mysteries of your present, and the potential of your future."

As Lauren peered into the pool, she saw visions swirling within its depths—images of her childhood, her moments of doubt and triumph, and the dreams she had yet to embrace. The crystals seemed to resonate with each vision, sending ripples of energy through her being.

"I see a soul who has walked the line between light and darkness," The Seeker said, their voice echoing through the cave. "You are a weaver of dreams, a keeper of mysteries, and a seeker of truth."

Lauren felt a sense of vulnerability and empowerment intertwining within her—a realization that her journey was not about being confined to one aspect of herself, but about embracing the multidimensional nature of her being.

The Seeker led her deeper into the cave, where a grand chamber awaited—a celestial wonderland of crystals that seemed to stretch to the heavens. The air was charged with energy, and Lauren felt a profound connection to the crystals that surrounded her.

"This chamber is where your journey truly begins," The Seeker said, gesturing to the walls adorned with crystals. "Each crystal holds a lesson, a revelation, and a gift. Choose the crystals that call to you, and they will become your allies in the quest for self-discovery."

Lauren carefully examined each crystal, sensing their energies with her intuition. She chose a shimmering rose quartz—an embodiment of love and compassion, an amethyst—a symbol of spiritual awakening, and a powerful obsidian—a talisman of protection and transformation.

With her chosen crystals in hand, Lauren felt a surge of energy coursing through her veins. She understood that the Enchanted Crystal Cave was not just a physical place—it reflected the depths of her soul, a sanctuary of self-awareness and growth.

The Seeker guided her to a tranquil alcove within the cave, where a crystal altar awaited. Lauren placed her chosen crystals on the altar, feeling a sense of communion with the universe.

"The crystals you have chosen are attuned to your essence," The Seeker said. "They will guide you on your journey, offering insight and support as you embrace the unique tapestry of your being."

As Lauren closed her eyes, she felt a profound connection to the crystals—their energies intertwining with her own. She saw visions of her past, her experiences, and her dreams, all merging into a kaleidoscope of colours and emotions.

In that moment, she understood that her journey of self-discovery was an ever-evolving symphony—a dance of light and shadow, of vulnerability and strength, and of embracing both her rock star vampire spirit and her mystical, intuitive self.

With the guidance of the crystals and the wisdom of The Seeker, Lauren knew that she would continue to explore the depths of her soul, unveiling the layers of her being, and embracing her uniqueness with an unyielding grace.

As the Enchanted Crystal Cave echoed with the song of her heart, Lauren's journey of self-discovery expanded beyond the confines of time and space. She had embarked on.

An odyssey of empowerment and enlightenment—a journey that would shape her destiny and inspire others to embrace the magic within themselves.

Deep within a forgotten forest, where the sunlight struggled to penetrate the thick canopy, lay the entrance to a mysterious crystal cave. Legends spoke of its magical properties, capable of granting unimaginable power to those who dared to tread its hallowed halls. As our hero ventured into the darkness, the air crackled with ancient energy, and the walls shimmered with ethereal light.

Within the depths of the cave, they would uncover long-lost secrets and discover their true potential in a world teetering on the brink of chaos.

5

The Enigmatic Prophecy

In the weeks that followed her transformative journey through the Enchanted Crystal Cave, Lauren returned to her everyday life in Barry Island. The memories of the mystical realm and the guidance of The Seeker continued to linger in her heart, like a melody she couldn't forget.

The crystals she had chosen at the cave became her constant companions. The rose quartz reminded her of the power of love and compassion, the amethyst nudged her towards spiritual awakening, and the obsidian protected her on her path of transformation.

As autumn painted the world with hues of gold and amber, Lauren found herself drawn to the cemetery once again. The silence and serenity of the place offered her solace and a connection to the past. She strolled among the tombstones, her fingertips grazing over the weathered engravings as if reaching out to the souls of those who had gone before her.

In the distance, she noticed a figure seated on a bench—a woman with silver hair that cascaded like a waterfall. Her eyes were filled with wisdom, and Lauren felt an inexplicable pull towards her.

"Hello, dear," the woman said, her voice soft and melodious. "I've been expecting you."

Lauren approached the woman, feeling an unspoken familiarity. "Have we met before?" she asked, her curiosity piqued.

The woman smiled knowingly. "In a way, we have," she replied. "I am Elara, a guardian of the spirits who reside in this sacred place."

Lauren's heart quickened, sensing that Elara held the key to unlocking even deeper mysteries. "What brings you here?" Lauren asked, intrigued.

Elara gestured to the surrounding tombstones. "I have always been drawn to the stories of those who rest here—their joys, their sorrows, and the legacies they are left behind. In these stories, there is wisdom to be found, and a reminder that life is a tapestry of both light and shadow."

As the days turned into weeks, Lauren and Elara spent many evenings together, sharing tales of the departed and the lessons they had left for the living. Through these stories, Lauren discovered that embracing one's shadows was just as important as celebrating one's light.

Elara's presence became a source of comfort for Lauren, a guide on her journey of self-discovery. The older woman's words echoed in her mind, reminding her that life was not just about pursuing the extraordinary—it was about finding beauty in the ordinary and finding strength in vulnerability.

One evening, as they sat together under the silver glow of the moon, Elara shared a story that touched Lauren's soul—the tale of a young woman who had been consumed by her fear of the shadows within.

"This young woman," Elara began, "feared that the darkness within her would overshadow the light, so she tried to bury her shadows deep within her heart. But in doing so, she denied herself the opportunity for growth and self-acceptance."

Lauren listened intently, recognizing aspects of herself in the young woman's struggle. Elara continued, "It was only when the young woman embraced her shadows, accepted them as part of her, that she discovered the true essence of her being—a powerful, multifaceted soul capable of extraordinary things."

Tears welled in Lauren's eyes as she realized the profound truth in Elara's words. She, too, had been avoiding her shadows, fearing that they would overshadow her strengths. But now, she understood that the journey of self-discovery was not just about celebrating her rock star vampire spirit—it was about embracing her vulnerabilities and finding strength in her unique tapestry of light and shadow.

In the days that followed, Lauren dove deeper into her art and creativity. She began to paint not only the vibrant and whimsical but also the dark and contemplative. Her canvas became a reflection of her soul, capturing the dichotomy of her being—a tapestry of colours that celebrated both her pink girly nature and her rock star vampire spirit.

Her photography took a new turn as well. She explored the beauty of decay—the withering petals of a flower, the fading light of the setting sun, and the impermanence of all things. Through her lens, she found a sense of peace in embracing the transience of life—a reminder that every moment held its own magic, whether in light or shadow.

As the seasons changed and winter enveloped Barry Island, Lauren's journey of self-discovery continued to unfold. She attended gatherings with friends and family, where she shared her newfound wisdom with those who sought guidance on their own paths.

Her masquerade balls became renowned events, drawing people from all walks of life. Each ball was a celebration of authenticity—a tribute to the power of embracing both light and shadow, of finding unity in diversity.

One chilly winter evening, as the moon hung low in the sky, Lauren found herself standing at the cliff's edge once more. The wind tousled her hair, and the sound of crashing waves filled the air. In that moment, she felt a sense of gratitude for the journey she had undertaken—a journey that had led her to discover the magic within her and to celebrate her uniqueness without hesitation.

She knew that the road of self-discovery was a lifelong one—a symphony of growth and transformation that would lead her to unforeseen destinations. With her heart filled with courage and her spirit ablaze with determination, Lauren embraced the shadows and the light within her, knowing that she was an

---

extraordinary being—an ever-evolving rock star vampire with a heart of gold.

As the moonlit night enveloped the ancient forest, Lauren found herself standing before the mysterious oracle. The cryptic words of the prophecy echoed in her mind, leaving her with more questions than answers. Determined to unravel the enigma and discover her true purpose, she embarked on a perilous journey into the heart of the unknown.

With each step, the weight of destiny pressed upon her shoulders, urging her forward. Little did she know that the tales of past and present would intertwine, revealing secrets that would shape her path and lead her closer to her ultimate calling.

6

Tales of Past and Present

As winter slowly melted into the tender embrace of spring, Lauren found herself drawn to a quaint little bookstore that had recently opened in the heart of Barry Island. The sign outside read, "Aurora Books & Curiosities," and she felt an inexplicable pull towards the shop.

Upon entering, the scent of ancient parchment and the soft glow of candlelight enveloped her senses. The shelves were lined with books of various genres, each one whispering its own story. Lauren meandered through the Isles, feeling as though the books were calling out to her.

In a corner of the store, she spotted a peculiar book—a leather-bound tome adorned with mystical symbols and intricate designs. Its title, "The Symphony of Souls," seemed to echo through her being, beckoning her to unravel its secrets.

Curiosity got the better of her, and she approached the counter, where an old man with a twinkle in his eyes stood. He introduced himself as Mr. Hawthorne, the proprietor of Aurora Books.

"Ah, I see you've found 'The Symphony of Souls,'" Mr. Hawthorne said, a knowing smile gracing his lips. "That book holds the tales of those who have walked the path of self-discovery—a symphony of souls that spans across time and space."

Lauren's heart quickened as she handed him the book. "Is it a collection of stories?" she asked, her curiosity piqued.

"In a way, yes," Mr. Hawthorne replied. "But it is also a reflection of the journey you have undertaken—a tapestry of experiences that resonate with your own quest for self-awareness."

With the book in her hands, Lauren felt a sense of anticipation. She knew that the pages held tales of souls who had embraced their uniqueness, just as she had, and she longed to discover the wisdom they had to offer.

As she began to read, she was transported to distant lands and far-off realms, where extraordinary beings grappled with their shadows and celebrated their light. Each story mirrored aspects of her own journey—of courage in the face of uncertainty, of growth through vulnerability, and of the magic that resided within.

In one tale, she read about a young woman who had an insatiable thirst for knowledge. Driven by a hunger to understand the world around her, the woman embarked on a journey of exploration—a quest that led her to the far corners of the earth.

The young woman faced challenges and obstacles along her path, but her tenacity and curiosity carried her through. In her pursuit of knowledge, she discovered not only the mysteries of the external world but also the depths of her own soul.

Lauren's heart resonated with the woman's story. She saw reflections of herself—the endless curiosity that had driven her to explore the realms of art, photography, and spirituality. She realized that her journey was not just about seeking external experiences; it was about delving into the mysteries of her own being.

In another tale, she read about a musician who had lost their ability to create music. Burdened by self-doubt and fear of failure, the musician had withdrawn from the world, unable to find the melody within.

Through a series of serendipitous encounters, the musician encountered a mentor—a wise sage who taught them the power of embracing imperfections and allowing vulnerability to flow through their music.

As Lauren read the musician's story, she felt a profound connection to her own struggles with creativity. She remembered moments of doubt and self-criticism, and she realized that her journey was not just about creating art—it was about finding the courage to share her creations with the world, imperfections, and all.

With each tale she read, Lauren discovered that the symphony of souls was not just a collection of individual stories—it was a grand symphony that wove together the threads of humanity, creating a tapestry of interconnectedness.

She understood that her journey of self-discovery was not a solitary one. It was a part of a greater symphony—a dance of souls, each playing their unique notes in the cosmic melody of life.

As spring blossomed into full bloom, Lauren found herself sitting by the cliff's edge once again. The sun dipped below the horizon, casting a kaleidoscope of colours across the sky. The crashing waves below seemed to echo the symphony of souls she had read about.

In that moment, she felt a sense of oneness with the universe—the understanding that her journey was a harmonious part of the greater whole. She embraced her pink girly nature and her rock star vampire spirit, knowing that both aspects were essential notes in the grand symphony of her life.

With a heart full of gratitude and a soul ablaze with inspiration, Lauren closed the book and returned it to Mr. Hawthorne. She knew that her journey of self-discovery would continue, with each chapter bringing new melodies and harmonies into her life.

As she bid farewell to the bookstore, she realized that the symphony of souls extended beyond the pages of a book. It was a living, breathing melody that echoed through the hearts of all beings.

---

a celebration of uniqueness, a dance of vulnerability, and a testament to the power of embracing one's true self.

As she walked back home, the moon shone down upon her, and Lauren felt a profound sense of serenity. She knew that her journey was far from over, but she was no longer afraid of the shadows that loomed in her path.

With her heart as her compass and her soul as her guide, she embraced the symphony of her life—a symphony of light and shadow, of pink girly dreams and rock star vampire spirit—a symphony that would resonate through the ages and inspire others to dance to the melodies of their own souls.

In the realm of forgotten memories and lost tales, Lauren delved deep into the annals of time. Ancient manuscripts whispered their secrets as she pored over their fragile pages, connecting the dots between past and present. The tales of heroes and heroines, of triumphs and tragedies, unfolded before her eyes, painting a vivid tapestry of human existence.

Guided by the whispers of those who came before, Lauren began to understand the intricate web of fate that bound her to this quest. With newfound knowledge, she set forth, ready to face the challenges that lay ahead.

7

Whispers Across the Ages

As the days grew longer and the warmth of summer embraced Barry Island, Lauren felt a newfound sense of purpose and clarity. The symphony of souls she had encountered in the pages of "The Symphony of Souls" had ignited a spark within her—a symphony of inspiration that pulsed through her veins.

With her heart as her guide, she embarked on a mission—to share the magic of self-discovery with the world. She organized workshops and gatherings, inviting people from all walks of life to explore their own unique tapestries and embrace the symphony of their souls.

The first workshop was held in a quaint community centre, adorned with vibrant paintings and crystals. Lauren's friends, family, and curious souls from Barry Island gathered, their eyes gleaming with anticipation.

"Welcome, dear friends," Lauren began, her voice resonating with warmth. "Today, we embark on a journey—a symphony of self-discovery, where we celebrate the light and the shadows within us."

As she spoke, she shared her own experiences—the trials and triumphs of her quest for authenticity, the challenges she faced, and the wisdom she had gained along the way. Her vulnerability touched the hearts of those gathered, inspiring them to embrace their own journeys of self-awareness.

Through art, meditation, and heartfelt conversations, the participants explored the nuances of their souls. They delved into the depths of their passions, their fears, and their dreams, unearthing the symphony that resided within each of them.

In the days that followed, word of Lauren's workshops spread like wildfire. People from neighbouring towns and distant lands travelled to Barry Island to be a part of the transformative experience she offered.

The community centre soon became a hub of inspiration—a sanctuary where souls could gather, explore, and celebrate their uniqueness. The walls filled with paintings, photographs, and written reflections—a tapestry of voices echoing the symphony of souls.

Lauren's workshops took on a life of their own, expanding beyond the confines of a single community centre. She held gatherings in meadows, forests, and even on the shores of the glistening sea. Each workshop was a celebration of life, of self-discovery, and of the magical bond that connected all beings.

The magic of the masquerade ball found a new home in these gatherings. People adorned themselves with masks and costumes, not to hide their true selves, but to celebrate the myriad facets of their beings.

One warm summer evening, Lauren hosted a particularly special gathering—the Symphony Unleashed Ball. It was an ode to the symphony of souls that danced in harmony with the universe.

As the sun dipped below the horizon, the ballroom filled with laughter and joy. Dancers twirled and spun, their masks gleaming in the moonlight. The air was alive with energy—a symphony of emotions, dreams, and aspirations.

Lauren stood at the centre of the ballroom, surrounded by the shimmering souls she had touched through her workshops. With a microphone in hand, she addressed the crowd.

"Tonight, we celebrate the symphony of our souls," she said, her voice strong and unwavering.

"Each one of us carries a unique melody—a song that resounds through the ages, connecting us to the stars and the cosmos."

The ballroom erupted in applause, and Lauren felt an overwhelming sense of gratitude. She knew that her journey of self-discovery had not only transformed her life but had also touched the lives of countless others.

As the night wore on, Lauren danced with friends, strangers, and kindred spirits. She felt a profound sense of unity—a connection that transcended time and space. In that moment, she understood that the symphony of souls was not just an individual journey—it was a collective dance of humanity.

The Symphony Unleashed Ball became an annual tradition, drawing people from all corners of the world. It was a testament to the power of embracing one's true self and celebrating the magic that resided within.

As the seasons changed and another year passed, Lauren's journey of self-discovery continued. Her workshops evolved, taking on new dimensions and reaching even greater heights of inspiration.

She travelled to far-off lands, spreading the message of authenticity and self-empowerment. She connected with people from diverse cultures, understanding that the symphony of souls was a universal language that bridged the gaps between hearts.

Back in Barry Island, the community she had nurtured thrived—a vibrant tapestry of souls who had found their own unique notes in the cosmic symphony.

One evening, as she stood on the cliff's edge, a gentle breeze caressed her cheeks. The moon shone brightly, and the waves below whispered ancient tales.

In that moment, Lauren felt a profound sense of fulfilment. She knew that her journey of self-discovery would continue, for it was an ever-evolving symphony that resonated through the ages.

With a heart full of gratitude and a soul set ablaze with purpose, she gazed up at the stars, knowing that each one held a story—a symphony of its own.

She smiled, realizing that her journey of self-discovery had no destination—it was a perpetual dance, a melody without end.

And so, Lauren embraced the symphony of her life—a symphony that celebrated the pink girly dreams and the rock star vampire spirit within her. She danced to the rhythms of her soul, knowing that she was a unique note in the cosmic symphony—an eternal song of love, light, and shadows.

A gentle breeze carried the echoes of distant voices as Lauren ventured into the mystical realm of whispers. Across the ages, the spirits of wise sages and forgotten souls spoke to her, their words like ethereal threads weaving a tapestry of guidance. They whispered of forgotten lands, hidden treasures, and ancient rituals that held the key to her true calling.

With each whisper, Lauren's purpose became clearer, her resolve strengthened. Embracing the power of the ages, she embarked on a journey infused with ancient wisdom, ready to embrace her destiny and unlock the secrets that awaited her.

8

The Symphony of Self

As the sun dipped below the horizon, casting its warm hues across the sky, Lauren found herself standing at the precipice of a new chapter in her journey on Barry Island. The waves lapped gently at the shore, a rhythmic reminder of the ceaseless dance of life. The symphony of souls that had accompanied her throughout her odyssey echoed softly within her, intertwining with the sea breeze that tousled her hair.

Gazing out at the expanse of the sea, Lauren's heartbeat in sync with the ebb and flow of the tides. The wisdom she had gained and the connections she had formed with kindred spirits had brought her to this pivotal moment. The knowledge that she carried a symphony of her own, a melody crafted from dreams, trials, and triumphs, filled her with both humility and purpose.

During this serene landscape, a sense of empowerment had taken root within her. Her workshops had become a beacon of light for those seeking to uncover their own symphonies. She had watched as people shed layers of self-doubt, each step a note in their own journey of self-discovery. The tapestry of unity she had woven with souls around the world painted a vivid picture of interconnectedness, reminding her that even in solitude, one is never truly alone.

As the time neared for her parents, Gill, and Nick to embark on their journey away from Barry Island, Lauren felt a mixture of anticipation and nostalgia. The nest that had nurtured her growth was temporarily emptying, and she saw it as an opportunity to embrace the lessons she had learned. Gill's voice echoed in her thoughts, a reminder to seek help when needed and to celebrate the contrasting shades of her identity—the delicate pastel dreams and the resolute rock star spirit.

Lauren stood at the train station on the day of their departure, their smiles reflecting both excitement and a tinge of wistfulness. Farewells exchanged; Lauren felt the weight of newfound responsibility upon her shoulders. Yet, intertwined with the challenge was an exhilarating sense of possibility, a chance to embrace her independence and further her purpose.

With each passing day, Lauren's symphony gained momentum. Her workshops evolved into transformative experiences, journeys into the heart of authenticity. The community on Barry Island flourished, its members resonating with the harmonious cadence of empowerment. Lauren nurtured connections with artists, musicians, and healers, each one contributing a unique note to the composition of shared dreams.

Collaboration became the thread that wove the tapestry of creativity, uniting minds, and hearts across diverse backgrounds. The spectrum of human experiences enriched the symphony, a celebration of the myriad ways in which individuals could harmonize with one another.

As autumn descended, Lauren's symphony expanded its reach beyond the shores of Barry Island. She embarked on a voyage of discovery, sharing her message across cities and villages. Her presence resonated deeply, igniting sparks of transformation in those who crossed her path. The symphony of empowerment and authenticity reverberated across landscapes, transcending geographical boundaries.

In each new setting, Lauren encountered souls who had weathered their own storms. Their tales of resilience and triumph became intertwined with her symphony, resonating as a testament to the indomitable strength within the human spirit. Every shared experience added depth to the symphony, a vibrant mosaic of stories contributing to the crescendo of empowerment.

Her travels brought her not only to diverse communities but also to ancient practices and timeless wisdom. Crystals whispered their secrets, energy healing unfolded its mysteries, and the interconnectedness of all life became a vivid reality. Lauren was a student of existence, absorbing the wisdom of the ages and channelling it into her symphony.

As winter painted the landscape with frosty hues, Lauren returned to the embrace of Barry Island. The familiar sights and sounds greeted her like old friends. This homecoming resonated as a testament to the symphony she had orchestrated, each note a reflection of the connections she had nurtured.

One crisp evening, Lauren found herself back at the edge of the cliff. The stars above winked like celestial notes in the grand symphony of the cosmos. The echoes of her journey whispered on the breeze, reminding her of the symphony of souls that had guided her. She took a deep breath, embracing the tapestry she had woven and the potential that stretched before her.

With the wisdom she had amassed and the empowerment she had ignited in others, Lauren's sense of purpose surged within her. She had learned to harmonize the contrasting elements of her identity, weaving them into a seamless symphony of self. This realization was her most profound revelation—a note of courage that had the power to transform her reality.

As the penultimate crescendo of her odyssey, this chapter marked a pivotal point in Lauren's journey. With newfound strength, she was poised to confront the malevolent force that threatened the mystical Isles. The echoes of her symphony intertwined with the wind, carrying a message of unity, resilience, and the boundless potential of the human spirit.

In this chapter of Lauren's tale, the symphony of self-rang out as a call to action, a crescendo of courage. It was a symphony that emanated from the heart of existence itself, inviting all souls to contribute their unique melodies to the harmonious dance of life.

And so, the symphony played on—a perpetual cadence that would reverberate through the ages, an embodiment of Lauren's journey, and a clarion call for all to embrace their own melodies. With the rising sun, Lauren knew that her symphony was far from complete, and she looked forward to the finale that awaited her—the grand crescendo of her magical odyssey.

In the grand tapestry of existence, Lauren's journey had woven threads of inspiration and courage, creating a symphony that echoed across time and space. The melodies of her experiences had become harmonious notes in the cosmic composition, a testament to the infinite possibilities that lie within the human spirit.

As she stood on the precipice of this new chapter, Lauren was acutely aware of the power she held within her. The symphony of souls that had guided her was not just an abstract concept; it was a living force that resonated in every heartbeat, every breath. With each step, she added her unique notes to the ever-evolving symphony, contributing to the ongoing dance of life.

The symphony had become her guiding light, leading her through challenges and triumphs alike. It was a reminder that every experience, every emotion, was a note waiting to be played. And as she looked out at the vast sea before her, she understood that the symphony was not limited by the horizon—it stretched far beyond what her eyes could see, encompassing the dreams of kindred souls around the world.

The tapestry of unity she had woven continued to thrive in the community she had nurtured. The workshops had become more than gatherings, they were

---

sanctuaries where souls could explore their own melodies, where vulnerability was celebrated, and where the power of authenticity was felt by all.

The harmonious cadence of empowerment resonated through every interaction, a testament to the symphony of self that Lauren had embraced.

Her collaborations with artists, musicians, and healers had infused new layers of richness into the symphony. Each partnership was a harmonious duet, a chance to blend unique perspectives and talents into a seamless composition. And as the symphony resonated through different mediums and expressions, it became a universal language that transcended barriers and united hearts.

As autumn's embrace arrived once again, Lauren's symphony spread its wings beyond the familiar shores of Barry Island. Her journey took her to distant cities and remote villages, each step an opportunity to share the symphony's melody. In the eager faces of workshop attendees, she saw the reflection of her own journey—a reflection that carried the potential for transformation and growth.

In every corner of the world, she encountered souls who had weathered storms and emerged stronger. Their stories became intertwined with the symphony, creating a tapestry of resilience and hope. With each shared experience, Lauren felt the symphony's harmonies deepening, resonating with a power that touched the very core of existence.

Ancient practices and timeless wisdom revealed themselves as she traversed the landscapes of existence. Crystals held the energy of ages, offering guidance and healing. Energy flowed through her like a river, connecting her to the heartbeat of the universe. She had become a conductor of the cosmic symphony, channeling its melodies through her very being.

As winter's breath painted the world in frost, Lauren returned to the embrace of Barry Island. The symphony of her soul reverberated through the familiar sights and sounds, creating a comforting cadence that sang of homecoming. Each note she had played, each connection she had forged, was etched into the fabric of the island, a testament to the symphony's enduring presence.

Standing once more at the edge of the cliff, Lauren felt a profound connection to the stars above. The celestial notes twinkled with the promise of endless possibilities, each one waiting to be explored. The symphony of souls that had guided her on this odyssey echoed through her, reminding her of the interconnectedness of all life.

With the accumulated wisdom and empowerment, Lauren's purpose burned brightly within her. She had learned to harmonize the melodies of her past and present, creating a symphony that resonated with the power of authenticity. This realization was a note of strength, A melody that could transform fear into courage and doubt into determination.

With newfound resilience, she was prepared to face the shadows that threatened the Isles. The echoes of her symphony intertwined with the wind, carrying a melody of unity, resilience, and the boundless potential of the human spirit.

The symphony of self-resounded as a call to action, a crescendo of courage that urged all souls to join the dance of life. It was a symphony that emanated from the heart of existence itself, inviting everyone to contribute their unique melodies to the harmonious rhythm of the universe.

As the symphony played on—a perpetual cadence that would echo through the ages—Lauren's journey continued. With each new sunrise, she embraced the infinite possibilities that lay before her. The finale of her odyssey awaited a grand crescendo that would weave all the melodies, lessons, and connections into a breathtaking conclusion.

With hope in her heart and the symphony of self as her guide, Lauren looked forward to the final act of her magical odyssey—a harmonious resolution that would echo through time, inspiring generations to come.

In the depths of her soul, Lauren heard a symphony of self beckoning her towards transformation. Each note resonated with her true essence, urging her to shed the layers of doubt and embrace her inner strength. With courage as her guide, she embarked on a journey of self-discovery, unearthing hidden talents and dormant passions along the way.

The symphony swelled within her, harmonizing with the rhythm of her footsteps, as she embraced her true potential. With every choice, every decision, Lauren sculpted her destiny, becoming the conductor of her own symphony.

9

The Magical Odyssey

As the evening sky was adorned with a thousand twinkling stars, Lauren, our protagonist, found herself standing on the grand stage of an ornate concert hall. A sea of expectant faces gazed up at her, their hearts filled with anticipation. This night was a celebration, a tribute to the journey of self-discovery that had taken her to the farthest corners of the world and deep into the realm of her soul.

"Good evening, everyone, and thank you for being here tonight," Lauren began, her voice echoing warmth and sincerity. "Tonight, we are not just gathered to listen to a tale; we are part of a symphony—a symphony of dreams, hope, and the boundless potential that resides within each one of us."

As she spoke, a montage of her transformative journey flickered across a large screen behind her. From the pastel dreams of her childhood to the rock star spirit that emerged in her adolescence, each moment was captured in a mesmerizing dance of light and shadow.

"I used to think that being unique meant choosing one aspect of my personality over the other," Lauren continued. "However, this journey has taught me that true uniqueness lies in embracing every facet of our being—the light and the darkness, the dreams and the fears. It is in this dance of duality that we discover our authentic selves."

Her audience listened intently; their hearts open to the symphony of words flowing from Lauren's soul.

"Through the workshops and gatherings, I witnessed the power of vulnerability—the beauty of sharing our stories and connecting with others on a soulful level," Lauren shared, her eyes shining with passion. "We are all woven into the tapestry of life—a symphony of souls that reverberates through time and space."

She took a momentary pause, allowing her words to resonate within the hearts of her audience, then continued, "Each one of you is a unique note in this cosmic symphony—a note that contributes to the harmonious dance of life. Embrace your melody, for it is a song that only you can play."

The echo of applause filled the concert hall, and Lauren felt a surge of gratitude. Her journey had led her to this moment—a moment where she could inspire others to embrace their uniqueness and pursue their dreams.

"As I stand here tonight, I am filled with awe and wonder at the endless possibilities that lie ahead," Lauren confessed, her voice rich with emotion. "We are all composers of our own symphonies, and the world is waiting for us to compose our masterpiece."

Her gaze connected with each soul in the room. "Let us not be bound by the expectations of others or the limitations we place upon ourselves. Let us dare to dream, to explore, and to embark on the grand adventure of life."

As she spoke, the stage came alive with dancers, musicians, and artists from diverse backgrounds. They moved in perfect harmony, a living embodiment of the symphony of dreams that Lauren had envisioned.

"We are the dream-weavers, the architects of our destiny," Lauren proclaimed. "Let us build a world where authenticity and love reign supreme, where each soul is celebrated for the unique melody, it brings to the symphony of life."

The symphony of dreams swirled around her, carrying the hearts of the audience to distant realms of possibility. In that moment, they all felt a deep connection—a unity that transcended all boundaries.

As the night came to an end, Lauren stepped off the stage, her heart aglow with the knowledge that she had fulfilled her purpose. The symphony of souls she had encountered on her journey had not only transformed her life but had also become a guiding light for others.

In the following days, the story of Lauren's symphony of dreams spread like wildfire. People from far and wide sought her wisdom, attending her workshops and gatherings with hearts open to the magic of self-discovery.

She travelled to distant lands, spreading her message of empowerment and authenticity. From bustling cities to serene mountaintops, the symphony of dreams echoed, inspiring souls to embrace their uniqueness and live life to the fullest.

Back in Barry Island, the community she had nurtured thrived.
a tapestry of souls who had discovered their own symphonies and danced to the rhythms of their hearts.

As Lauren gazed out at the horizon, she knew that her journey was far from over. The symphony of dreams had become her life's work—a perpetual dance of inspiration and growth.

With every note, she found a new adventure, a new melody waiting to be played. With every step, she encountered new souls—kindred spirits who added their harmonies to her cosmic symphony.

As her story continues to unfold, it serves as a reminder that each one of us is a unique note in the grand symphony of life. Embrace your uniqueness, for it is the key to unlocking infinite possibilities.

Let your dreams guide you, for they are the North Star that will lead you on the path of purpose and fulfilment. As you embark on your own journey of self-discovery, remember that you are never alone. The symphony of souls resonates within and around you, celebrating the beauty of being human.

As the symphony plays on

---

a melody that knows no end—it will echo through the ages, inspiring generations to come.

And thus, with hearts full of hope and dreams reaching for the stars, let us compose our symphonies—a symphony of love, courage, and the indomitable spirit that resides within us all.

With this whispering journey ending, Lauren is ready for the next adventure in 'Whispers of the Dragon's Peak'. This new adventure will lead her to Dragon's Peak, where she will unearth an ancient alliance between dragons and humans, face a dark force threatening chaos, and must summon her courage to restore balance and preserve her ancestors' legacy. but had As the final pieces of the puzzle fell into place, Lauren's magical odyssey neared its climax.

Armed with knowledge, wisdom, and a heart filled with determination, she stood on the precipice of her ultimate purpose. The forces of darkness gathered, their shadows threatening to engulf the world. But within Lauren burned a spark of light, a beacon of hope that would guide her through the darkest of times. With allies by her side and the weight of destiny on her shoulders, she prepared to face the final battle, ready to fulfill her destiny and bring forth a new era of magic and wonder.

About The Authors

G.E. Dwynnigan

G.E. Dwynnigan is the creative collaboration of two talented authors, G and E, whose passion for storytelling and shared love for adventure and self-discovery brought them together.

G (Author G)

A Spirited Soul with a Welsh Heart. - Author G is a vibrant and spirited women, hailing from the charming town of Barry in South Wales. Growing up in this cozy Welsh community, she felt a deep connection to her roots, and the influence of the town's famous sitcom only solidified her Welsh identity. With an undying love for rugby, she's the ultimate supporter, and her passion for the sport is evident in her unwavering loyalty to her favourite team.

Author G's journey took an unexpected turn when she met her soulmate, N, who swept her off her feet with his charm and wit. Their love story led her across the border to England, where she embraced a new chapter of her life. Despite the distance from her homeland, Author G's Welsh spirit remains unyielding, and she takes every opportunity to celebrate her Welsh heritage.

In her professional life, Author G is a creative soul, working in counselling and therapy. Her warm and empathetic nature makes her a natural people person, and she finds joy in connecting with others and helping them on their own paths of self-discovery. When she's not immersing herself in the world of storytelling, Author G indulges in her love for nice food, exotic cocktails, and weekend getaways filled with new experiences. And let's not forget her beloved feline companion, Dory, the adorable fat cat who adds an extra dose of love and laughter to her life.

E (Author E)

A Philosophical Explorer with an Irish Heart. Author E is a free-spirited adventurer with a background in psychology. Hailing from the enchanting land of Ireland, he grew up with a deep appreciation for creativity and a love for exploring the unknown. Living life with spontaneity and embracing every opportunity that comes his way, Author E is the person you want by your side for unforgettable escapades.

His journey led him to Mexico, where he found a new home and immersed himself in its rich culture and beauty. As an avid scuba diver, he enjoys diving into the depths of the ocean, uncovering hidden treasures and marvelling at the wonders of the underwater world.

Author E lives with two faithful companions, Daithi and Dougal, his beloved dogs who share his zest for life and adventure.

In writing, Author E lets his creativity flow like a river, weaving tales that captivate and inspire readers to embark on their own journeys of self-discovery. He believes in the magic of storytelling and the power of imagination to transport readers to new realms of possibility.

About the Last Name "Dwynnigan"

The last name "Dwynnigan" is a mystical creation, blending elements of Welsh and Irish origins. It represents the magical synergy between the two authors, G and E, and reflects the enchanting worlds they bring to life through their storytelling. Like a secret key, the name "Dwynnigan" unlocks the door to a realm of imagination and wonder, inviting readers to embark on a symphony of dreams and discovery.

Together, G.E. Dwynnigan

Crafts stories that resonate with the human spirit, exploring themes of adventure, self-discovery, and the beauty of embracing one's uniqueness. Their collaboration blends the vivid Welsh charm of Author G with the psychedelic Irish spirit of Author E, resulting in a harmonious symphony of creativity that will leave readers enchanted and inspired.

So, buckle up for an extraordinary journey as G.E. Dwynnigan takes you on a rollercoaster of emotions, unveiling the magic that unfolds when two creative souls join forces to create something truly special.

Fantasy Book Reviews

Bookish Realm Magazine

"In 'Whispers of the Mystical Isles,' G.E. Dwynnigan conjures a breathtaking tapestry of magic and self-discovery. With a skilful blend of whimsical charm and dark intrigue, the story immerses readers into a world where the boundaries between reality and fantasy blur. Lauren's journey is a heartfelt exploration of identity, embracing both light and shadow—a testament to the power of self-acceptance. Dwynnigan's masterful storytelling transports readers on a thrilling quest, leaving them captivated until the very last whisper."

Fantasy Realm Gazette

"Prepare to be spellbound! 'Whispers of the Mystical Isles' casts a bewitching enchantment, blending the best of Welsh and Irish folklore into a riveting tale of magic and adventure. Dwynnigan's writing is an ethereal symphony, evoking vivid landscapes and unforgettable characters. Lauren's journey of self-discovery is a breathtaking odyssey, drawing readers into a world where mythical creatures and crystals hold profound significance. This enchanting debut captivates the heart and leaves readers yearning for more."

Bookworm's Haven Review

"G.E. Dwynnigan has crafted an exquisite tapestry of emotions in 'Whispers of the Mystical Isles.' The characters resonate with authenticity, and Lauren's journey of self-exploration is both relatable and empowering. Dwynnigan masterfully balances themes of identity, friendship, and destiny, painting a vibrant world filled with both light and shadows. The mystical Isles come to life in this captivating tale, as Lauren's connection with crystals and her mystical allies adds depth to the narrative. 'Whispers of the Mystical Isles' is an enchanting symphony of imagination and heart—a must-read for fantasy enthusiasts of all ages."

The Enchanted Reader's Journal

"G.E. Dwynnigan's 'Whispers of the Mystical Isles' is an enchanting ode to self-discovery and the magic within us all. Lauren's journey is a testament to the resilience of the human spirit, and readers will find themselves drawn into her world, yearning for the mystical Isles' secrets to reveal themselves. Dwynnigan weaves a mesmerizing narrative that seamlessly blends elements of Welsh and Irish mythology, creating a captivating and immersive experience. With every turn of the page, 'Whispers of the Mystical Isles' casts a spell, leaving readers under its enchantment long after the final chapter."

Coming Soon

Book Two: Whispers of the Dragon's Peak

In the second instalment of the series, "Whispers of the Dragon's Peak," the mystical Isles lead Lauren to a majestic mountain, hidden deep within the heart of Wales. Upon reaching Dragon's Peak, she uncovers an ancient alliance between the dragons and the people of the land. But as harmony unravels, a dark force threatens to unleash chaos upon the mystical Isles. With the fate of the dragons and the enchanted realm hanging in the balance, Lauren must summon her courage and form an unlikely bond with a wise dragon to restore the balance and preserve the legacy of her ancestors.

Book Three: Whispers of the Enchanted Forest

"Whispers of the Enchanted Forest" transports readers to the verdant landscapes of Ireland, where the mystical Isles reveal a hidden world brimming with magic and mischief. As Lauren ventures into the heart of the ancient forest, she encounters a mischievous leprechaun who guards a portal to the ethereal realms. Drawn into a high-stakes game of riddles and secrets, she must outwit the cunning leprechaun and decipher the clues to save the enchanted forest from an impending curse. Along the way, she discovers the true meaning of friendship and the magic of believing in the unseen.

Book Four: Whispers of the Castle's Legacy

In the next chapter of the series, "Whispers of the Castle's Legacy," Lauren finds herself in the quaint English countryside, where the echoes of history resound through the walls of an ancient castle. Within its hallowed halls, a legendary British bulldog guards a secret of immense power—one that could reshape the mystical Isles forever. Guided by whispers from the past, Lauren must unravel the castle's enigmatic legacy, confront the shadows of history, and tap into the essence of courage. As her journey comes full circle, she discovers that her destiny is intricately entwined with the enduring spirit of the castle and the soul of the mystical Isles.

www.ingramcontent.com/pod-product-compliance
Lightning Source LLC
LaVergne TN
LVHW052103160826
845678LV00015B/3340

* 9 7 8 1 4 4 6 7 7 5 3 1 8 *